How the Whale got his Throat

by Rudyard Kipling

Retold by Anna Milbourne

Illustrated by John Joven

Once upon a time, Whale was ever so greedy.

He ate scuttling crabs...

...and slow-moving starfish.

He ate great
big mackerels...

...and tiny
little snackerels.

He was so greedy, he swam around
eating anything and everything in the sea!

One clever little fish
hid behind his ear, so he
wouldn't be eaten too.

"If you're so hungry, why don't you eat
a man?" the clever fish suggested.
"Man is the very tastiest thing of all."

"Ooh, where can I get a man?" asked Whale.
"In fact, where can I get lots of them?"

"One will be enough, I'm sure,"
said the clever fish.

He showed Whale a man who was
bobbing along on a wooden raft.

Whale thrashed his great tail and swam close.
He opened his enormous mouth wider...
and wider... then...

GULP!

He swallowed the man, raft and all.

The man wasn't happy.

Inside Whale's belly,
    he danced and jumped...

...and banged
and bumped...

...and thrashed and thumped.

Until Whale groaned, "That hurts. Come out!"

"Take me to land first," called the man.

Thrashing his great tail, Whale swam and swam,
all the way across the wide, blue sea.

At last, he came to land.

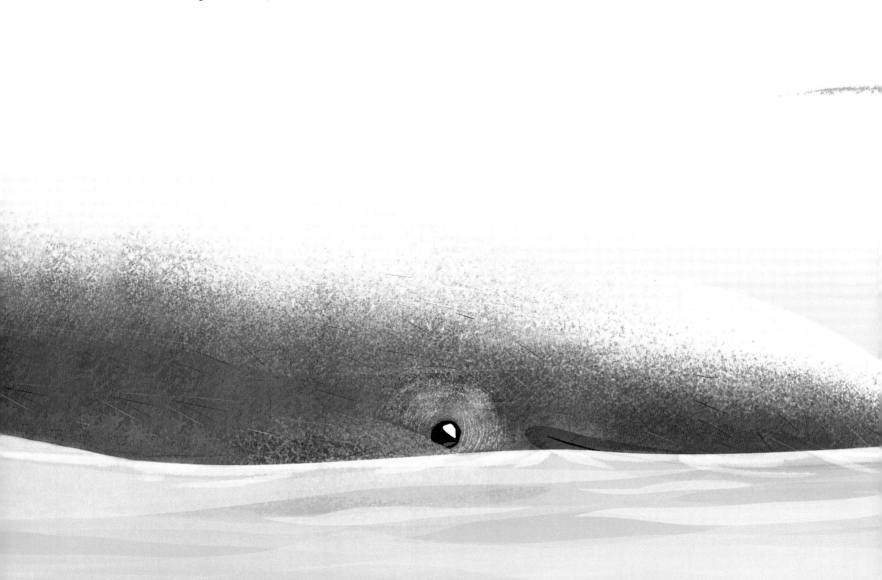

The clever little fish came too.

Inside Whale's tummy, the man was busy.
He cut up his raft...

...and made a big
criss-cross shape.

He wedged the criss-cross shape
deep into Whale's throat...

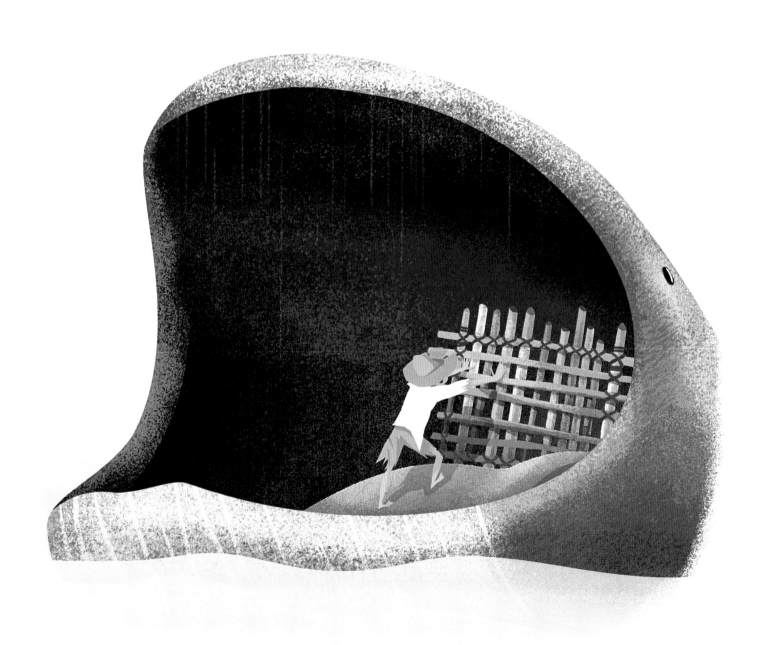

...and left it there when he jumped out.

"So long, Whale," he called.

Now Whale can only swallow tiny things.

He can't be greedy
any more.

How the Whale got his Throat is from the book
Just So Stories by Rudyard Kipling, which tells
stories of how animals came to be the way they are.

Edited by Lesley Sims
Designed by Sam Whibley

First published in 2016 by Usborne Publishing Ltd., Usborne House, 83-85 Saffron Hill,
London EC1N 8RT, England. www.usborne.com Copyright © 2016, 2015 Usborne Publishing Ltd.